PLAY BALL!

by Eric Howard
illustrated by Vicki Gullickson

Harcourt

Orlando   Boston   Dallas   Chicago   San Diego

Visit *The Learning Site!*

www.harcourtschool.com

They can play.

Zack is here now.

They pick it up.

What is in it?

Now they can play.

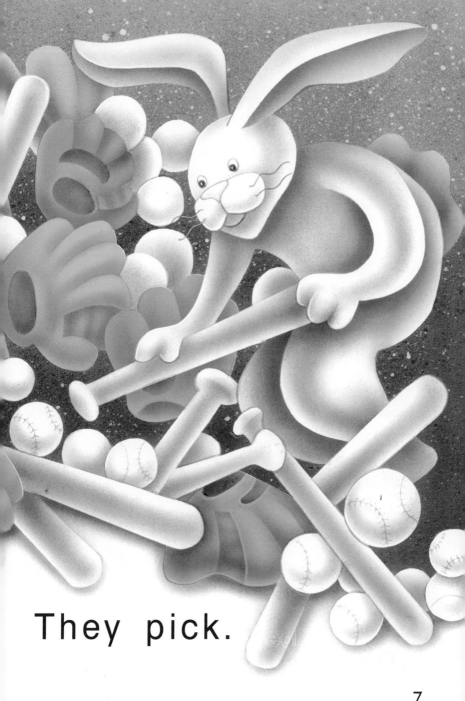

They pick.

Now they play ball!